Cornelius P Schermerhorn

Atomic Creation and other Poems,

Cornelius P Schermerhorn

Atomic Creation and other Poems,

ISBN/EAN: 9783741183805

Manufactured in Europe, USA, Canada, Australia, Japa

Cover: Foto ©Andreas Hilbeck / pixelio.de

Manufactured and distributed by brebook publishing software
(www.brebook.com)

Cornelius P Schermerhorn

Atomic Creation and other Poems,

ATOMIC CREATION

AND

OTHER POEMS,

BY

CORNELIUS P. SCHERMERHORN.

NEW YORK,

1883.

To my

esteemed friend

and fellow citizen,

Hon. Josiah Sutherland,

these Poems are

dedicated.

PREFACE.

Kind friend, gentle reader,
These poems to you I tender,
Hoping they will, on inspection,
Receive approval, approbation.

If not gems, brilliant or rare,
They may be worth reading with care,
In examining them at your leisure,
May afford both profit and pleasure.

If in these poems you should find,
On perusal food for the mind,
A thought worthy to treasure,
I shall be amply paid for my labor.

CONTENTS.

ATOMIC CREATION.

While of creation I sing,
  Invoke the muse's wonted fire,
To penetrate nature's scheme,
  My thoughts my pen inspire.

A theme wondrous, sublime!
  An undertaking bold;
To scan the depths of Time,
  Its doings to unfold.

Amid the realms of night,
  Ere orbs above did glow;
Before they took their flight,
  Or worlds evolv'd below.

Ere the sun shed its rays,
  Before the moon did beam,
Ere there came dawn or days,
  Atoms we trace—no being.

Footprints, there were none around,
  All was silent, drear,
No voice was heard, no sound
  There was, no revolving year.

Atoms, imperial reigned
  Amid space ; they strode
Within their vast domain,
  In solitude they rode.

Atoms did every where abound,
  Swiftly they whirl'd,
Until a rest they found,
  Amid a forming world.

Through boundless regions swept,
  To find their fellow mate,
Journeying, never slept,
  Traveling early, late:

Onward the atoms flew,
  Kindred atoms to meet ;
Came in numbers, not few,
  They fondly did greet.

In the atoms primal,
  Reside forces that draw,
That, to forming centres, travel,
  Obedient to law.

Amid depths abyssmal,
  They sped their way,
Drawn by forces rythmal,
  To where worlds in embryo lay.

Atom followed its fellow atom,
To nucleus far did hie,
Where they worlds did fashion,
Below, around, on high.

Roaming in myriad numbers,
Onward they did course
To their forming centres,
Whence evolv'd the universe.

In time's misty pages,
As we their traces scan,
In them read atomic doings,
How orbs evolv'd, and man.

Worlds in their order came,
Were from central nucleus thrown,
Cours'd mid fire and flame,
Mid cycles past, unknown.

Revolving centres were form'd
   Amid the depths of space,
From which worlds evolv'd,
   And ran their circling race.

By forces centrifugal,
   Orbs from nuclei were hurl'd,
They by forces centripetal,
   Around their centres whirl'd.

As on their axis they did roll,
   Satellites they unfurl'd,
They circled their axial pole,
   And thus evolv'd the worlds.

We mark their orbital course,
   As they did onward bound,
Those units of the universe,
   Traveling their annual round.

The orbs above that glow,
  They move in wondrous order;
We their orbital places de know,
  Their paths tracing ever.

The power that whirls the spheres,
  In primordial forces lay;
They have cours'd for untold years,
  From their circuits ne'er did stray.

This boundless temple of nature,
  In which worlds revolve ever,
By the laws of gravitation
  Are firmly held together.

Nature's imperial scales,
  Faultless, commit no error;
Thus order everywhere prevails
  Within the dome of nature.

Far beyond the milky way,
  Countless worlds do glide—
Mightier than the orb of day,
  Primal forces do them guide.

The orbs their places know,
  From them do ne'er depart ;
In order move, above, below—
  What skill, what wondrous art.

How far soe'er away,
  How numerous or vast,
Scales infallible did them weigh—
  They ne'er move too slow, too fast.

In forces elemental dwell
  The power that whirls them 'round,
Directs their paths so well,
  Their circuit to a moment *are performd* ~~profound~~.

Those primordial laws in matter,
    Guide all the orbs that roll;
The imperial scales of nature
    Balances the whole.

Since orbs began their course,
    And worlds in space were hurl'd
Amid the boundless universe,
    Harmonic order has prevailed.

Those atomic architects,
    Had endless time for building:
In their method are no defects—
    They primal laws obeying.

In their silent bound
    Have constructed a unique temple;
No error in their plans are found—
    With resources exhaustless, ample.

ATOMIC CREATION.

In those tiny builders
  Dwell the molehill, the mountain,
The dew drop that glitters,
  The rivulet, the fountain.

Ocean, with its weird refrain,
  Tall glaziers that in it glide,
Tidal waves that sweep the main,
  In atoms these reside.

The snow flake that descends,
  The meteors that flame,
The thunderbolt that rends—
  They from atoms came.

The diamond, its sparkling fire,
  The ruby, with its glow,
The pearl, the glowing sapphire—
  These gems atoms did bestow.

Comets that flame and burn,
 That roam in depths of space
For a thousand years, ere they return,
 To atoms these we trace.

The tender leaflet, the flower,
 The rose, with its perfume,
That adorns the bower,
 That corridors festoon.

The old forest oak,
 That withstood centuries of storm,
That time at length smote,
 Then the atoms did form.

The soft zephyrs that blow,
 The cyclone that whirls
O'er the ocean, and lo,
 Ships beneath are hurl'd.

Heaven's fork'd lightning,
  That sweeps across the sky,
Denizens of earth frightning,
  In atoms these forces lie,

The condor, mounting high,
  The smallest insect that flies,
The eagle from his eyry,
  Far off his prey descries.

From tiny germ to massive mastodon,
  That once roamed the earth,
Atoms did form, did fashion,
  It to all life gave birth.

All worlds from atoms came,
  Mid the cycles that ran ;
The orbs passed through fire and flame,
  Before life on them began,

Man, with his imperial brain,
  Who scans the distant spheres,
On earth supreme doth reign,
  Evolv'd from atoms, mid the years.

While of orb and systems I sing,
  And forces that them sway,
Will not now dwell on organic being,
  But on solar worlds that near us lay.

The planets that roll in marvelous order,
  Around the mighty orb of day;
He guides their pathway ever—
  None from him do stray.

Apollo did them hurl—
  Into space was thrown;
He them around did whirl—
  They were children of his own.

First, Neptune, with his trident, courses
   Around the central sphere,
Guided by imperial forces,
   In one hundred eighty years.

Next Georgium Sidus came,
   Six moons this world doth light;
Around the glowing orb of flame,
   In ninety years performs his flight.

Saturn, god of Time, five rings him adorn,
   Eight moons do light his course;
In thirty years his round performs,
   Amid the solar universe.

Jupiter, fourth and monarch of the worlds,
   But Apollo doth him guide and sway;
In twelve years around him whirls—
   Four moons do light his way.

Mars, deck'd in war's grim visage,
  Fifth in the planetary race,
Alone performs his entourage,
  No moon to light this orb, we trace.

Earth next his journey makes
  Around the central orb ;
A single year his circuit takes—
  One moon doth light this world.

Venus, brilliant, bright and fair,
  Next courses in regal splendor ;
To this queen of beauty rare
  The orbs court do render.

Mercury, last and least of the planets.
  That around Apollo sweep—
No moon doth light his circuit—
  Unlit his path he keeps.

Spheres between Mars and Jupiter are seen,
 These around ~~high~~ *bright* Phœbus glide;
On them he doth radiant beam,
 Their circuit doth prescribe.

All these the central orb obey,
 He guides their pathway ever;
They ne'er from him can stray,
 Or from each other sever.

The Sun, with his train of worlds,
 Circles the imperial alcyone;
In eighteen million years he whirls
 Around this astral dome.

On those spheres that roll around
 The imperial orb of day,
Air and oceans do abound,
 And fork'd lightnings play.

Seasons that unfold verdure,
　Fragrant flowers that bloom ;
Springtime, summer, winter,
　Evening, twilight, morn, high noon.

On those revolving spheres
　Myriad beings dwell,
That came with the coursing years—
　None their forms can tell.

While I have sang of solar orbs
　That around Apollo glide,
Let me sing of sidereal worlds,
　That far away reside.

As we view yon dome of stars,
　That glow in radiant splendor,
The light that came from those orbs afar,
　Many years in space did wander.

Light, with its rapid flight
  Of twelve million miles a minute,
Ere a ray from the nearest reach our sight,
  Ten years hath sped ere our orb doth visit.

Yon bright star, Centauri,
  Before its light on earth did beam,
For twenty years in space must fly,
  Ere by mortal eye 'tis seen.

As we view yon sidereal orb Cigni—
  The ray that left its starry home—
Before it did reach our eye,
  Fifty years in space did roam.

We behold the stellar panorama,
  Its far off brilliant dome,
The light that left Cappalla
  For earth, a hundred years had flown.

The rays that glow from Arcturus,
   Whose speed outruns the lightning—
Before it courses to us,
   Two hundred years was traveling.

The polar star, the mariner's guide,
   Its rays that reach his eye at night,
His bark to steer o'er ocean's tide,
   Was five hundred years in flight.

The imperial orb, Alcyone,
   So distant is it from our world—
The light that left its far-off home
   For earth, a thousand years had whirl'd.

Yon brilliant star, Sirius,
   So remote is it in space,
If Sol revolv'd so far from us,
   His light we ne'er could trace.

Myriad suns there are,
   Circling vast centres round,
Whose rays are lost in ethereal air,
   Amid depths of space profound.

Stellar orbs revolve, whose light
   For million years did roam,
With its winged arrow flight,
   Have not yet reached our solar home.

Pond'rous spheres beyond "the milky way"
   Around mightier orbs do glide ;
On other worlds their light display,
   Before they reach earth, fade.

Suns course beyond suns, and further on,
   There arise in endless succession
Other suns, that around other centres run
   And orbs and systems unending.

As from them we take observation,
　　From either side of earth's orbital base,
Scarce an arc of variation
　　In the visual lines we trace.

Earth had sped two hundred million miles away
　　From where the first view was taken ;
At this distance the lines parallel lay,
　　They not a second subtending.

Such the marvelous depths of creation—
　　None can it know or scan ;
Defying all mensuration,
　　All powers of imperial man,

Before it we stand appalled,
　　Lost in silent wonder ;
None the empyrean heights have solv'd,
　　Or depths of this dome of nature.

As we have sang of distant spheres,
   Their unfolding from atomic matter,
Amid the ever circling years,
   Let us view organic life that came later.

When earth into space was hurl'd,
   It revolv'd an orb of flame ;
For cycles 'twas an igneous world,
   Before life on it there came.

A firey sphere it roll'd,
   Around its centre cours'd :
No life it did unfold
   Amid a forming universe.

In solitude it whirl'd around
   The central orb of fire ;
No life on it was found—
   All was silent, drear.

It revolv'd for ages long,
　　Amid the solitudes of night;
No voice was heard, no song—
　　Silent it sped its flight.

For cyles 'twas a flaming mass,
　　Coursing around its centre,
The ages that rolled past,
　　None can know or number.

Its flames at length grew dim,
　　It roll'd an orb of flame no more,
Its glowing fires retir'd within,
　　Vapors dense did upward pour.

Its central fires fiercely raged,
　　Earth's surface was rended, broken,
Streams of lava o'er it surg'd,
　　Of life there was no token.

Water came to its depths, retir'd,
   Rivers cours'd by unseen,
Earth, sombre and unattir'd,
   Unfolded no being.

Vapors that upward rose,
   Return'd in falling rain ;
A hardening surface earth did disclose,
   But still no life there came.

Storms o'er earth did glide.
   Tidal waves lav'd its shore,
Sol, unseen, o'er the heavens did ride,
   Earth's fires were seen no more.

The stars above did glow,
   Earth was wrapp'd in vapors dense,
His rays did not pass the mist below,
   For many ages hence.

When earth's vapors did ascend,
  Revealing the azure skies,
Rare beauty it did lend,
  But not to mortal eyes.

The moon shed its silvery light,
  Arcturus did brightly beam,
There was none to view the sight,
  On earth there was no being.

Hills arose, and mountains,
  Valleys, but no verdure,
Lakes appeared, and fountains,
  But no organic creature.

Islands upheav'd, 'mid ocean
  Thunders loud did roll,
The elements were in commotion,
  From near to farther pole.

Showers, gentle dews there fell,
  The earth was deck'd in green,
Cloth'd the dale and dell,
  But there came no being.

This orb for life at length was fitted,
  For ages long it did prepare,
Constituents of life was segregated
  In its waters, land and air.

It to life at last gave birth,
  A formless germ there came,
'Twas life, it sprang from earth,
  Without function, form or name.

This life that on earth 'rose,
  We in the rocks do trace,
They to us disclose
  The type whence sprang the race.

As coursing Time swept on,
  Amid earth's granite pages,
In the epoch huron,
  We behold life's upward stages.

In the Laurentian strata,
  Species protozoan are seen,
And Rhizopods, at this data,
  A higher type of being.

Advancing in the organic scale,
  In earth's age salurian,
The molusk did prevail,
  And the order crestacean.

Trilobytes fill'd the ocean,
  New species of in.vertebrate there came,
The brachiopods were in motion,
  In its seas did long remain.

ATOMIC CREATION.

Life, in changing forms, went on,
  As the cycles cours'd by,
In earth's epoch, devonian,
  We a higher type descry.

Vertebrates in this era came,
  Fishes of the ganoid order,
They in its ocean long did reign,
  Of hetrocertal type and structure.

As we trace life onward, later,
  Species reptillian were found
In earth's age triasic, and after
  This, order did abound.

The icthysaurs its seas did roam,
  With telescopic eye and rapid sweep ;
Monarch in his ocean home,
  His victims caught, did eat.

As life we upward trace,

    As it rose in the scale organic,

New types there came apace,

    Birds appeared in the age oolitic.

In earth's period, jurassic,

    It great Saurians did unfold,

The dinosaurs, in form titanic,

    And massive, we behold.

Later in the epoch miocene,

    Mammalian quadrupeds did roam,

The huge mastodon, magatherium,

    And mammoth made earth their home.

They on it roamed for ages,

    Trod its firm surface o'er,

When in later tertiary stages

    They sank beneath to rise no more.

New forms of life evolv'd apace,
   They, in time, gave place to others,
Better fitted for the race,
   To meet life's rude encounters.

In the world's age pliocene,
   The order, quadrumana, rose,
A still higher type of organic being
   A later period did disclose.

So life arose in the organic scale,
   In its progressive bound,
Until man it did unvail
   In the posttertiary age was found.

For ages long earth did prepare,
   Its soil it cloth'd with verdure,
With oxygen supplied the air,
   For this last noblest work of nature.

Life in various forms had risen,
    In numerous types appear'd on earth,
None the time computing,
    Before it to man gave birth.

Man stood the highest type of life,
    That arose amid the ages,
Since its dawn and strife,
    The rocks reveal the stages.

The lowest forms are found below,
    As we trace the organic mould,
And to earth's surface go,
    The highest types unfold.

In ocean's upheav'd strata,
    The dead lay pil'd in mountains deep,
Of this tomb of life we have no data,
    Of the myriad that there do sleep.

O'er this mausoleum of the past,.
  Of earth's countless dead . .
That perish'd 'mid cycles vast,
  The living do o'er them tread.

From this organic tomb
  Our marble palaces we build,
Their massive corridors and domes
  With tablets moulded from the dead are filled.

As new environments arose on earth,
  From subsidence of land or water,
It to other forms of life gave birth,
  And they to others, later.

So life conform'd to earth's conditions,
  Old types did disappear,
Others arose with new functions,
  On this ever changing sphere.

Amid ages of contending strife,
In its waters, on its land,
There arose myriad forms of life,
Until man on earth did stand.

When primitive man appeared,
He had no habitation,
He no temples rear'd,
Had no weapons for protection.

He roam'd on earth a nomad,
The caves were his abode,
Unkempt and unclad,
'Mid forest depths he strode.

As onward we man trace,
This denizen of caverns,
This prototype of our race,
Constructed rude dwellings.

Far back in ages prehistoric,
   He weapons had invented,
Him to shield from carniverous visit,
   To caves no more resorted.

In the stone ages there did abound
   Structures on piles driven,
In them utensils for use were found,
   Footprints of a dawning civilization.

As centuries onward rolled,
   In the bronze age was seen
How primitive man did unfold
   In the scale of organic being.

The massive structures of this age
   The modern do surpass,
What toiling millions did engage
   In rearing those edifices vast.

They huge and ponderous stand,
 Old Time did o'er them sweep,
Beneath those structures grand
 Their unknown builders sleep.

They are lost to historic fame,
 None their times or age can tell,
Their sepultures reveal no names,
 When they on earth did dwell.

Artists of ancient fame, renown,
 Ocean o'er their works did sweep,
Before its tidal wave went down,
 They lie beneath the deep.

Rare works of art and sculpture,
 That in ages past arose,
Have disappeared, sank under,
 Coming time may them disclose.

The arts that buried lie,
  Future man will unearth, unfold,
They will astound the artist's eye,
  When he their beauty does behold.

Those works of the unknown past,
  That old Time has swept away,
Ornate temples, obelisks vast,
  May yet behold the light of day.

They future villas will adorn,
  Their statues on public plazas stand,
Modern art of its fame be shorn
  By the works of an unknown hand.

In Egypt's forty dynasties we trace
  How man mentally had risen,
The arts of this ancient race
  Revealed a high civilization.

Her temples massive, grand,
  Of artistic mould and sculpture,
As before those mighty works we stand,
  We gaze in mute wonder.

Her obelisks, her catacombs,
  Sepultures in which her princes slumber,
Her pillars, palatial domes,
  The reign of her regnal sovereigns number.

Imperial cities of unrivalled splendor,
  Her pyramids colossal, *tall*
The gorgeous ruins of Carnac Luxor,
  We reverent before them fall.

Her pyramids to us reveal
  How the sciences she did unfold,
The laws of nature did unseal,
  From those observatories of old.

For astronomical purposes erected,
   The planetary motions to trace,
Here their orbital times were calculated,
   As they revolv'd 'mid space.

To commemorate the round of the pleiades
   The pyramid cheops was erected,
Requiring a period of ten thousand decades,
   To return from whence they started.

It also signalled the conjunction
   Of the planetary spheres,
A phenomena not again occurring
   In o'er five thousand years.

As coursing Time swept on,
   The arts advanced apace,
In the Grecian parthenon,
   We its matchless beauties trace

In her far-famed Attica,
    The highest art did unfold,
The temples of Theseus, Minerva,
    We with mute awe behold.

This rude city of Crecopia,
    That to such eminence had risen,
The statues of Jupiter, Diana,
    Are the world's admiration.

She gave birth to philosophers, sages,
    Who nature's problems did scan,
Whose aphorisms adorn the ages,
    Thus arose primitive man.

As we onward trace civilization
    To Rome, that to vast power arose,
She unfolded orators, statesmen,
    And warriors that slew her foes.

Her civilians gave law to the world,
　　Her orators thundered in the forum,
Their anathemas on the enemy hurl'd,
　　With her armies swept o'er them.

This great commonwealth of Rome,
　　So massive in its structure,
Its institutes, its musty tomes
　　Will adorn the ages ever.

This power that ruled the nations
　　Arose from a rude beginning,
It unfolded a mental cerebration,
　　Subsequent time not excelling.

Rome, no longer on her seven hills,
　　Does sovereign o'er the nations reign,
She no more hurls her legions,
　　Her power departed, not her fame.

As time did onward bound,
　　We trace advancing civilization,
Until modern man is found,
　　Harnessing the lightning.

The elements his behests subserve,
　　Become his servants on ocean, land,
They from duty ne'er do swerve,
　　Ever obedient to command.

His orders they faithful keep,
　　Traveling to places distant,
O'er the globe they sweep,
　　Conveying messages in an instant.

Annihilating time and space,
　　Remote regions are brought near,
Vast distances effaced,
　　On this revolving sphere.

Inhabitants on this solar orb,
   Resident at either zone, '
Converse in speech or word,
   As if they were at home.

We have traced man's upward stride,
   From where rude and primitive he lay,
To where the lightning he guides,
   And the elements him obey.

How came he lord on this earth ?
   At the head of organic nature,
When so tiny at his birth,
   To rise o'er it imperator.

Environing forces man did impel,
   Amid ages of contending strife,
Imperial on earth to dwell,
   O'er all forms of organic life.

This mental power in man,
　　Was by countless ancestors transmitted,
It through myriad numbers ran,
　　Amid cycles vast integrated.

'Tis the segregated force of ages,
　　Of progenitors countless in number,
Before there were historic pages,
　　In unknown graves they slumber.

Man's massive cerebration,
　　Gave to him his mental force,
By which he rose to his present station,
　　At the head of the organic universe.

None can penetrate or scan,
　　This mental unfolding of the race,
The time through which it ran,
　　No one can compute its space.

ATOMIC CREATION.

There are races who in the mental scale
  Are so feeble in their grasp and girth,
That cycles of time would scarce avail
  Them to rise to highest types on earth.

Will man still higher powers attain ?
  Advance in the mental scale,
His future place on earth's domain,
  Coming time will alone unveil.

The future man we cannot know,
  What earth has for him in store,
Whether he will higher go,
  Or disappear, be seen no more.

Worlds may in time grow old,
  Lose their embryotic force,
They no more will life unfold,
  Amid the solar universe.

They into central fires may fall,
    Their atoms whirl'd in space,
New orbs from them unfurl,
    And other beings evolve apace.

It may be the primal law of worlds,
    That from atoms were segregated,
That they to central fires should whirl,
    To nebula again be relegated.

Integration and disintegration
    Are elemental forces in matter,
Are the conservators of creation,
    Preserving its temple ever.

Thus worlds unfold, dissolve,
    As the cycles onward course,
New orbs from the old evolve,
    Amid an unfolding universe.

In the far nebula we behold
  Myriad orbs that glitter,
And nuclei that worlds unfold,
  And life in the ages after.

In yon constellation, Orion,
  As we with aided vision penetrate,
Orbs appear, numbering millions,
  And worlds in embryotic state.

'Mid the streaming "milky way,"
  As we its depths pursue,
Countless spheres their light display,
  By telescope brought to view.

How far soc'er with it we sweep,
  · Myriad orbs before us rise,
Radiant, in form replete,
  Dazzling to mortal eyes.

So worlds unfold, evolve,
   Amid this vast dome of nature,
We the distant nebula resolve,
   Suns are reveal'd in countless number.

As we view yon stellar dome,
   Its myriad flaming spheres,
Some have left their starry home,
   Within known historic years.

Stars that once did glow,
   No more this orb they light,
Are not seen on earth below,
   They are lost to solar sight.

On us they no longer beam,
   Have fled into depths of space,
Their light is gone, unseen,
   We it no more can trace.

They so far away have flown,
   On their siderial round,
For million years will roam,
   Ere they circle their astral round.

Some have left, others unfold to view,
   Earth has just received their light—
What depths of space did they pursue,
   How vast their orbital flight.

Yon orbs that glow with fire,
   That other worlds do warm and light,
And them for life in time prepare,
   As they perform their orbital flight.

No life on them could dwell,
   While they are orbs of flame
No one the time can tell,
   When life on them will reign.

But the spheres that round them whirl,
  That they do light and warm,
They life will evolve in turn,
  As they their rounds perform.

Worlds will evolve life sooner, later,
  As they course their annual round,
Amid the dome of nature,
  Life will on them be found.

Countless orbs there are in space,
  That for life are being fitted,
Others in their orbital race,
  With the elements of life have parted.

On some glowing fires still burn,
  Others have lost their heat, grown cold,
In solitude their circuits run,
  They life will no more unfold.

ATOMIC CREATION.

Stellar suns may cease to glow,
  Part with their radiant fires,
No longer warm the orbs below,
  Then life on them expires.

Planets may grow old, decrepit,
  Lose their elements, air, water,
For life be no longer adapted,
  Lifeless will roam hereafter.

The moon, a barren orb, doth course,
  Silent, it whirls around ;
Water, air, life's only source,
  No longer on her are found.

Sol, his fires may lose, may wane
  Amid the cycles that roll,
When life will cease on earth's domain,
  Become a waste from pole to pole.

But the stream of life will ever flow,
　Amid the myriad worlds that course,
Around, above, below,
　Amid the boundless universe.

Nature, that to life gave birth,
　That evolved from atomic matter,
Must return to its mother earth,
　To the bosom of its alma mater.

The womb of life to replenish,
　Nature's offspring to her must return,
That the race may not perish,
　That the stream of life may go on.

Our magna mater we greet,
　For her children she doth care,
At her table provides a seat,
　Loaded with viands rare.

This great mother we hail,
  Her distributions are large,
Her bounties ne'er fail,
  Howe'er extensive her charge.

While partaking of her store,
  Should remember the giver,
To the bonntiful bestower,
  Tribute should render.

When our feast of life is o'er,
  And we silent return to nature's bosom,
Of her larder will partake no more,
  But bask in her font lethean.

Nature hath love for her own,
  She will desert her offspring never,
She has built for them a home,
  Will guard it sacred ever.

She has erected her temple,
  Filling boundless space,
Has made provision ample
  In it for all the race.

Its massive corridors resound
  With the myriad that in them tread,
Through them roam, and lo, are found
  Among the sleeping dead.

Other guests this temple enter,
  Its broad aisles do echo
With the footsteps of the untold number
  That in them come and go.

No habitat of this dome can tell
  The number that beneath do rest,
That in it once did dwell,
  Entomb'd they lie on mountain crest.

This muasoleum of all the dead,
　　Is the repose of organic strife,
None from it have fled,
　　None have risen to life.

Its denizens oblivious lie,
　　They hear not heaven's thunder,
Ne'er feel a pang of grief, or sigh,
　　In it will ever slumber.

Nature is life's womb and tomb,
　　She to all being gave birth,
That dwell or rest beneath this dome,
　　Since first it sprang from earth.

The architect of this dome of nature,
　　The countless worlds in space,
Life that will continue ever,
　　To nature's God we trace.

This temple adorned with imperial man,
　Imbued with mental force sublime,
That was garnish'd as the cycles ran,
　'Mid abyssmal depths of time.

In this boundless temple of creation,
　Man has but a brief tenure,
Marks not a line in time's mensuration,
　An unknown factor in earth's population.

A waif on life's ocean toss'd,
　On its bosom drifts, goes under,
Amid its depths he is lost,
　Is seen no more forever.

An atom in a shoreless universe,
　As he sinks beneath the tide,
May leave a ripple in its course,
　That down the centuries will glide.

NIAGARA.

The majestic waters of Niagara
  In their deep refrain,
Descending do not tarry,
  But hie to the main.

Its echoes none did hear,
  As they were upwad hurl'd,
They fell upon a silent sphere,
  Upon a voiceless world.

Its mighty waters in their fall,
Wore gorges deep and tall,
Their path there were none to trace,
Or mark their slow but tireless pace.

Niagara from its heights did bound,
On Ontario's shore resound,
Upward moved to Eric's crest,
No pause, it knew no rest.

Its titanic waters that descend,
In artistic beauty blend,
They to the ocean glide,
To mingle with its flowing tide.

But not in ocean depths to stay,
In tiny streamlets wend their way,
Again from rockey heights to pour,
But farther from Ontario's shore.

It vapors in clouds arise,
They vail the azure skies,
Its rainbow visitors delight,
With its pendants tall and bright.

The pond'rous waters of Niagara,
Wore chasms deep and craggy,
They from dizzy heights did pour,
But nearer to Lake Erie's shore.

Since Niagara began her roar,
It through walls of granite tore,
Its forces none could stay,
They paused not night nor day.

Amid ages vast, remote,
Its herculean waters smote,
The rocks were riven, broken,
Of man there was no token.

Onward they sped their course,
Amid a silent universe;
Man came, heard their echoes deep,
Them could not lull to sleep.

Since Niagara's roar began,
None the time can scan,
We in its rocky pages find
The distance left behind.

A channel deep it wore,
For seven leagues or more,
Onward coursed its way,
. To where above Lake Erie lay.

The boasted works of man,
Pigmies before Niagara stand,
Mute we behold and silent,
Nature's forces eloquent.

Niagara, its weird refrain
Has echo'd for cycles unknown,
Its power symbols the people's reign,
The tyrant's rule o'erthrown.

The mighty thunders of Niagara

Emblem the forces of democracy,

Before which thrones do fall,

Monarchs and despots all.

THE RED MAN.

In western climes did roam
    The red man tall and brave,
The forest was his home,
    His requiem the wave.

O'er sylvan stream he glided
    Swiftly, with his canoe,
Arrows him food provided,
    " Envy nor ambition knew."

He raised not stately domes,
    His temple the blue sky,
Erected no altars, thrones,
    Unsepultured he lies.

He waged no aggressive war,
  His hunting-grounds defended
Against robbers from afar,
  Who them wantonly invaded.

The red man of the forest
  The continent roamed o'er,
Tall and brave has sank to rest,
  Beyond Niagara's roar.

Sons of those sires remain,
  Feeble and few in number,
Driven from their domain
  By vandals for plunder.

They had possess'd for ages,
  This heritage of their fathers,
Not recorded in titled pages,
  But unjustly seized by robbers.

The gods who rule above
　　Will vindicate the right,
Nations chastise, reprove,
　　Who for spoils war and fight.

For those forest braves we sigh,
　　They worship'd not in altars,
But under the azure sky
　　Sang their orisons and psalters.

They have gone to their island home,
　　To return again, no, never,
Their hunting grounds no more will roam,
　　Freed from their despoilers ever.

NOT A WASHINGTON.

———

'Mid time's weird epochs,
There were monarchs and despots,
Heroes, orators, statesmen,
There was no Washington.

Empires had risen, fallen,
Old time swept o'er them,
Entomb'd lie her great sons,
Among them no Washington.

There were philosophers, sages,
Who adorn'd the ages,
Men of wisdom, penetration,
But there came no Washington.

Egypt, with her obelisks, domes,
Her pyramids and catacombs,
Kings repose in her mausoleums,
And princes, but no Washingtons.

Troy, that fell before her Grecian foes.
Whose walls at Apollo's lyre rose,
Had Hector, and other valiant sons,
But they were not Washingtons.

Balbeck, of prehistoric fame,
Her granite walls still remain,
They reveal an ancient civilization,
But unfolded no Washington.

Carthage, on Afric's far shore,
Founded by Dido, now no more,
Had Hannibal, an illustrious son,
Famous in war, not a Washington.

Ancient Tyre, Corinth, Sidon,
Cities of commercial renown,
Had Hiram, other eminent sons,
But they were not Washingtons.

Thebes, with her massive grandeur,
Her columns we behold with wonder,
On them are inscrib'd her noble sons,
They record no Washingtons.

Syracuse, with her towers tall,
'Mid the punic wars did fall,
Had Archimedes, a famous son,
A mechanician, not a Washington.

Palmyra, that armies swept o'er,
Had Zenobia, in days of yore,
With Longinus, a favorite son,
A savan, not a Washington.

Athens, with her temples stately,
Of Theseus, Diana, Minerva,
Had Solon, Pericles, worthy sons,
They were not Washingtons.

Rome, who ruled the world,
O'er all climes her legions hurl'd,
Had her Scipios, Cæsars, brave sons,
But they were not Washingtons.

Mexico, with her effete millions,
Fell before Cortez' legions,
Had her Montezumas, Gautemozon,
Patriot sons, but not Washingtons.

Europe, that for centuries had slumber'd,
Awoke, produced heroes unnumber'd,
Had her Nelsons, Wellingtons, Napoleons,
Valiant sons, but not Washingtons.

America, that for ages untold,
Was unknown to the rest of the world,
Had an ancient, unique civilization,
But as yet there came no Washington.

At length Columbus, a son of Genoa,
Arose, gave birth to fair Columbia,
She in time brought forth an unrival'd son,
The incomparable Washington.

He immortal will live in fame,
The ages will revere his name,
'Mid the world's great and illustrious sons,
There was but one, one only, Washington.

A REPUBLIC.

Centuries had roll'd by,
  Empires arose unnumber'd,
People for republic did sigh,
  While in chains they slumber'd.

They had waited for it long,
  While in fetters they were bound,
At last resolv'd to right the wrong,
  A republic to found.

Twas on Columbia's shore,
  That freedom first awoke,
'Twas heard in the cannon's roar,
  When the tyrants they smote.

The roll-call sounded at Bunker Hill,
    The patriots did rejoice,
The colonial heart did thrill,
    'Twas freedom's stern voice.

'Twas not for fame, renown,
    They met the enemy on battle field,
Until Britain's flag went down,
    To patriot arms did yield.

The colonial heart did glow,
    When victory they had won,
From a haughty, tyrant foe,
    By the immortal Washington.

This freedom our sires won,
    'Twas wrested from Britain's grasp,
Here a republic broad was laid,
    That shall for ages last.

THE FLAG.

On Columbia's far shore,
A banner was waving,
Where cannons did roar,
Aloft it was streaming.

For liberty it wav'd,
For it heroes contending,
Amid conflict it gleam'd,
O'er the dead, the dying.

Riven, tatter'd and torn,
O'er battle fields streaming,
Onward 'twas borne,
Brave sons it defending.

Borne upward and onward,
   'Till the foe vanquish'd, yielding,
Washington had conquer'd,
   The enemy surrend'ring.

Patriots beheld with delight
   Their flag proudly waving,
O'er the victory for right,
   While Brittons lay trailing.

Our sires their freedom won,
   From the tyrant foe wresting,
Gave to America its boon,
   A republic creating.

This emblem of freedom,
   O'er a nation waving,
Upheld by brave freemen,
   In battle never trailing.

This bright starry banner,
 A union of States symbolizing,
To all despots a terror,
 The world, in arms, defying.

Ægis of a sovereign people,
 To it nations are flocking,
No foe on it dare trample,
 No aggressor escaping.

Flag of the brave, the free,
 Its citizens protecting,
Wherever it waves, on land or sea,
 'Tis beheld with rejoicing.

This flag our fathers won,
 'Mid conflict long and trying,
Bequeath'd from sire to son,
 It never surrendering.

May it wave unblemish'd,
  Its stars brightly beaming,
With its lustre undiminish'd,
  Their numbers increasing.

This flag of the brave and the free,
  Sons of our sires ne'er dishonoring,
O'er the world may it wave,
  Liberty and justice maintaining.

NAPOLEON.

Like a flaming meteor rose,
    Deck'd in war's grim visage,
Hurling destruction on his foes,
    Has ended his entourage.

With lightning force he smote ·
    The nations around him,
However distant, remote,
    His legions swept o'er them.

The towering Alps he bestrode,
    Like Hannibal, the Carthagenian,
O'er Italy's plains he rode,
    Scattering the foe before him.

This intrepid warrior bold
  To Egypt extended his sway,
Under the mighty pyramids of old
  The fierce Mamelukes did slay.

He o'erthrew mighty kingdoms,
  The world beheld with wonder,
This hero with his legions,
  Subduing armies without number.

The forces of Prussia and Russia
  Combined to o'erthrow him,
At Friedland and Auderstadt, Jena,
  With his legions he smote them.

Emperors united their forces,
  At Austerlitz resolved to crush him,
With his marshalls and legions,
  Like an avalanche swept o'er them.

With his forces hitherto invincible,
  He march'd to Russia's frigid zone,
The Czar Alexander to humble,
  And hurl from his throne.

At Smolensk and Borodino he conquer'd,
  Drove Kutozoff and his Cossacks before him;.
Arctic waters his legions environ'd,
  Spread destruction around him.

This meteor thunderbolt of war,
  That shot athwart the horizon,
Saw in his ill-fated star
  His invincibility departing.

At Waterloo he essayed to regain
  The throne whence he was driven,
Imperial once more to reign,
  The suppos'd favorite of heaven.

The morn of Waterloo's eventful day,
　　Napoleon for the battle eager,
'Tis the sun of Austerlitz, did say,
　　He before night was a prisoner.

The conflict raged 'mid fire and flame,
　　Napoleon exclaimed, "the battle's won,"
Blucher to Wellington's rescue came,
　　'Twas lost, Napoleon was undone.

This mighty incarnation of war,
　　His path strew with desolation,
O'erran states and empires afar,
　　Has fulfilled his mission.

He has fought his last battle,
　　He with his legions together slumber,
The cannon's roar, the bayonet's rattle
　　Will arouse the warrior never.

Napoleon dead still lives,
His fame will descend the ages,
His name, imperishable, will survive,
'Mid time's indestructible pages.

THE RIGHTS OF LABOR.

As on toiling couch I lay,
  Scanning the heavens o'er,
To myself did silent say,
  What hath life for me in store.

I view'd the glowing orbs above,
  Beaming with beauty bright,
Symbols of power and love,
  That orders all things right.

Those shining orbs proclaim
  A potent force that guides,
That supreme doth reign—
  Whence those tears and sighs.

Nature has adorn'd her temple,
　　Her gifts did equitably bestow,
Made provision for all ample,
　　Why starving multitudes below.

Her children to her are equal,
　　She endow'd none with privilege,
While man on his neighbor tramples,
　　Despoils him of his heritage.

Our bounteous alma mater
　　For her offspring did provide,
While man robs man of his labor,
　　Listen to the rumbling tide.

Justice hath long slumber'd,
　　While the oppressor rioted in spoil,
His days of pelf are number'd
　　On freedom's sacred soil.

The people who sovereign reign,
　　Will vindicate the right,
Those depriv'd of their rightful gain
　　Are marching in force and might.

Their footsteps loud we hear,
　　A resistless spartan band,
Their oppressors well may fear,
　　When the oppress'd their rights demand.

Your spoils must surrender,
　　The people have so decreed,
They a verdict just will render,
　　Which the oppressors well may heed.

BE CHEERFUL.

As we journey through life,
  Ne'er despond on the way,
Bravely meet its ills and strife,
  There will dawn a brighter day.

Be cheerful and happy,
  Not repine under sorrow,
Be content, if not merry,
  Hope for a better to-morrow.

Keep your eye on the goal,
  If misfortunes o'ertake you,
Know no such word as fail,
  Again try, the gods will help you.

They will assist those
   Who put their shoulder to the wheel,
Not lie in inert repose,
   But try with cheerful zeal.

The gods bestow their favor,
   To the deserving give,
Will reward honest labor,
   The worthy their aid receive.

Then toil with cheer, be merry,
   'Twill bring its own reward,
Those in the end are truly happy
   Whom with favor the gods regard.

ART VERSUS NATURE.

Who can paint the flowers?
  Their blendings so exquisite,
Birds of plumage 'mid the bowers,
  Art can but imitate.

The rose, so radiant, so ruddy,
  Its hues to transfer to canvas,
With its inimitable beauty,
  It all art doth surpass.

Art with nature cannot vie,
  She hath wrought so lovely
Her tints that adorn the sky,
  What artist can them copy?

To paint Sol's azure light,
That gilds the mountain,
Her golden rays so bright,
Or the sparkling fountain.

The whirling cyclone, the storm,
O'er land and ocean sweeping,
The meteor that flaming falls down,
The thunderbolt, the lightning.

The colors of the rainbow,
The diamond and sapphire glowing,
To these art must reverent bow,
They all art transcending.

The ocean's crested wave,
The streamlet's gentle gliding,
Glaziers, that seas do lave,
That tall ships are stranding.

Cascades from high that fall,
    The dewdrops of the morning,
Phœbus, that shines for all,
    To paint these all art defying.

Will art the beauties of nature attain,
    As art is advancing?
Unfold a limner, a fame,
    All former artists surpassing.

Nature o'er art, her superior,
    He who for perfection in art is striving,
Must study the great master, nature,
    If he would her be rivaling.

ODE TO THE SUN.

———

Thou radiant orb of day,
   Whose fires ceaseless glow,
That pond'rous spheres doth sway,
   Around, above, below.

Dost thou sovereign o'er them reign,
   Thy fires light and warm them all,
Within thy solar domain,
   Planets great and small?

Those mighty forces, are they thine?
   Kindling fires that ceaseless burn,
That on revolving spheres do shine,
   That around thee whirl in turn.

Is this wond'rous power thine own,
   That keeps the orbs in course,
That marks the time that they perform
   Their circuits 'mid the universe.

If not thy own, whence the power
   That myriad spheres do guide,
That marks the time, the hour
   That they around vast centres glide?

'Tis a force, a power unseen,
   Resides potential in matter,
In nature it reigns supreme,
   No power higher, greater.

This primordial force in nature,
   Evolv'd worlds, made their fires to glow,
Unfolds the orbs that move in order,
   'Mid the universe above, below.

This power all worlds doth sway,

   It moulded suns, lit their fires,

Gave us the radiant orb of day,

   To thee we offer pæans, prayers.

THE WINDS.

The winds in their nestling home,
  Quiet when in slumber,
Arous'd with fury roam,
  Become a rattling thunder.

With titanic power they sweep,
  Tall forests lie prostrate, riven,
Navies are stranded in the deep,
  By the fierce storms of heaven.

They sweep o'er sea and land,
  Destruction marks their course,
Naught can them withstand,
  Herculean is their force.

The paths of commerce do bestride,
   Carry destruction in their path,
As they onward glide,
   In their cyclonean wrath.

When in repose so gentle,
   By zephyrs onward borne,
Arous'd how terrible,
   Riding the crested storm.

Those azure winds of heaven,
   Who doth them control?
By what forces are they driven,
   From near to farther pole.

Boreas, from his northern home,
   To southern realms doth fly,
Auster, from his southern dome,
   Northerly doth hie.

Euras, from the east courses his way,
To western climes he wends,
Zephyrs in his gentle sway,
A soft'ning influence lends.

In the caves of Eolus are held
The winds when in repose,
He doth them loose and wield,
Sparing neither friends nor foes.

In his imperial chambers are bound
Those mighty forces of nature
That circle the globe around,
He guiding their path ever.

THE ELOQUENCE OF SILENCE.

———

The falling tear, the speaking eye,
The throbbing heart, the heaving sigh,
Those silent utterances we hear,
Excels all form of speech whate'er.

As kindred hearts together meet,
Silently they each do greet,
They feel an innate thrill,
That words cannot reveal.

The earnest, silent prayer
In closet, where'er we are,
More eloquent than spoken art,
It melts, it sinks into the heart.

A silent monitor within,
Voiceless and unseen,
Reclaims the wayward youth
From vice to virtue, truth.

No eloquence of speech or word,
Such reclaiming powers afford,
An innate moving force,
An imperial, silent voice.

Amid the solitudes of night,
Ere Knox had winged her flight,
As on silent couch man lay,
Plans matur'd that empires sway.

He who the sceptre wields,
In state or tented field,
'Twas not by speech he gain'd
His powers, or reigned.

THE ELOQUENCE OF SILENCE.

The man of brains who plann'd,
All factors weigh'd and scann'd,
'Tis silent thought that rules,
Not the eloquence of schools.

The sun with its radiant light,
With its swift winged flight,
The stellar orbs that glow,
Beam silent on earth below.

The depths of old ocean
Feel not tidal commotion,
Remain calm 'mid the storm,
O'er its surface waters borne.

Rivers to the ocean noiseless glide,
To mingle with its flowing tide,
Return in silent showers of rain,
The fields to clothe with waving grain.

The planets voiceless roll,
Around their orbital pole,
Their silent forces are not heard,
More eloquent than speech or word.

The power that whirls the mighty spheres,
For countless, unknown years,
Is noiseless and silent,
Voiceless, but eloquent.

The potent forces in nature
Have been working silent ever,
The rythm of the myriad spheres
Are music to list'ning ears.

The snowflakes that descend
In artistic beauty blend.
The rain drop, the pearly dew,
Silent, arid earth renew.

The loves of organic nature,
Silent woo, speak never,
They voiceless mate and wed,
Noiseless approach the nuptial bed.

The eloquence of silence is gold,
Its power is unsung, untold,
The man of silent thought and brain,
He sovereign will rule and reign.

TIME, AND THE LOST ARTS.

———

Time, in its ceaseless bound,
  On its fleet coursers,
Circles its round,
  Naught can stay his forces.

The years pass, are gone,
  In the ocean of time fall,
Others swiftly come,
  Its depths garners all.

'Mid time's vast flight,
  The arts were unfolded,
They became lost to sight,
  With the artist who moulded.

The lost arts of old
  Will again appear,
Coming man will them behold,
  Their graces admire.

Works long since buried,
  That time swept away,
Their excellencies will be studied,
  When they see the light of day.

Art, that went under,
  Some savan will reveal,
The future artist will wonder
  At their artistic skill.

Those works that buried lie,
  Coming time will restore,
When they meet the artist's eye,
  Their beauty will adore.

Arts of the prehistoric past,
 That have been hidden so long,
Their time and age lost,
 To the surface will be borne.

So modern art in its bound,
 To time must surrender,
In future ages may be found
 The artist who wrought never.

Time and art march together,
 As the years roll apace,
Time art will sweep under,
 With its matchless grace.

Lost art future villas will adorn,
 Her statues on public plazas stand,
Modern of its beauty will be shorn,
 By the works of an unknown hand.

ODE TO THE OCEAN.

Ocean, thy weird refrain,
   Long echo'd o'er a silent world,
No life in thy depths there came,
   Cyclones o'er thee whirl'd.

Thy waters lav'd the mountain side,
   They mark thy tidal stages,
Ere man did o'er thy bosom glide,
   Or scann'd thy rocky pages.

Thy waves for ages swept
   Amid the solitudes of night,
'Mid abyssmal depths they slept,
   None to behold their towering height.

Countless years pass'd away
   Since their refrains began,
There was no dawn, no day,
   When thy tidal waves first ran.

None can compute the years
   That o'er thy bosom have cours'd ;
No philosopher, savan, seer,
   'Mid depths of time they are lost.

Thy waves no more silent fall
   Upon yon mountain side,
Ships sweep o'er thy bosom tall,
   The wealth of nations on thee glide.

Couldst thou thy treasures reveal,
   That beneath thee lie buried,
What wealth they would unseal,
   That thy waves have garner'd.

In thy depths what teeming life,
  That in them sport and roam,
Myriads have perish'd in the strife,
  Have built our marble homes.

As we o'er thy bosom glide,
  Below lie pil'd the myriad dead,
That in the ages past have died,
  The coming man will o'er them tread.

They for cycles long have lain,
  Have mass'd to mountains deep,
When they tower above the main,
  Thy waters will not o'er them sweep.

Will thy refrains continue ever,
  As the cycles sweep along?
Thy tidal waves mount higher,
  And echo louder thy weird song.

THE MOUNTAIN LAKE.

Beneath yon mountain crest,
   A sylvan lake lay embower'd,
In the forest depths did rest,
   Tall trees its bosom mirror'd.

Storms above it swept,
   Fowls on its waters did glide,
In quietude it slept,
   Below the mountain side.

Birds carol'd 'mid the bowers,
   But their notes silent fell,
There were none to gather the flowers,
   That grew in the lonely dell.

In its sequestered home
   This lake had for ages slumber'd,
O'er it man did not roam,
   But fish sported unnumber'd.

This repose was at last broken,
   Its habitats footsteps did hear,
An arrow sped, to them a token
   That some enemy was near.

Those waters in their calm quiet,
   On them no voice or sound was heard,
Until the red man did them visit,
   Nought but the forest bird,

This sylvan lake mirror'd o'er,
   That had lain in repose so long,
The fowl or red man are seen no more,
   Its shores echo the woodman's song.

THE COTTAGE NEAR THE SEA.

I built a cottage for my fair,
   Down near the deep, blue sea,
For my lassie with golden hair,
   I met under the willow tree.

She beheld the crested wave,
   From her cottage near the shore,
Some mariner deign'd to save,
   When storms did fiercely roar.

The music of the waves she heard,
   As they swiftly cours'd along,
The notes of the ocean bird,
   That echo'd o'er the storm.

The chimings of the old ocean,
  With its weird refrain,
To her symbol'd a devotion
  To the ruler of the main.

In this sea-girt home,
  With my lassie so sweet,
Ne'er from it will roam,
  While my darling there I greet.

My lassie with the golden hair
  I met under the willow tree,
So angelic and so fair,
  We ever one will be.

Pride of the ocean, the valley,
  With her rich, waving tresses,
A form so petit and fair,
  It all others surpasses.

Guardian angel of the ocean,
  Gliding o'er the crested wave,
'Mid tempest, what devotion,
  Some lost mariner to save.

In our cottage near the sea,
  With its ever-flowing tide,
With my lassie, with thee
  Will henceforth reside.

Should ocean sweep our cottage o'er,
  We would be borne on its tide,
To yon lethean shore,
  There to rest side by side.

TO LOUISA.

My darling Louisa,
    Thee I adore,
Let's hie to some charming villa
    On the sea-girt shore.

Our bark gently wafted
    Amid islets fairy,
Under azure sky canopi'd,
    With my dearest Louisa.

Borne by zephyrs o'er the tide,
    Inhaling the fragrant air,
As 'mid the flowers we glide,
    With my Louisa, the fair.

The port we would enter,
As onward we sail,
In it ride at anchor,
Secure from the gale.

In this sequester'd villa,
'Mid its roses and flowers,
To roam with my Louisa,
What bliss would be ours.

In this paradise of beauty,
In this sea-girt isle,
To dwell with my Louisa,
To bask in her smile.

In this Elysiam so fairy,
Amid the deep blue sea,
With my ador'd Louisa,
We ever one would be.

ROSEVALE.

On the banks of the Hudson,
   'Mid dell and dale,
We behold a quaint mansion,
   'Tis called Rosevale.

Tall forest o'er it waving,
   Whose branches arch'd meet,
Its scenery so charming,
   Its roses so sweet.

Erected before the Revolution,
   It a lone monument doth tower,
Of the merciless iconoclasm
   That by it did pour.

Near this ancient home repose
　　Sires and sons who in it did dwell,
Whose ancestors met our tyrant foes,
　　They rare feats of arms did tell.

Denizens of this old county seat,
　　Sitting in its piaza, or green moor,
Received news of Washington's retreat,
　　Heard the cannon's fierce roar.

And the loud peals of thunder.
　　That roll'd o'er the wave,
When Washington had conquer'd,
　　His country did save.

Let this grand old mansion
　　That witness'd events so thrilling,
Be sav'd from destruction,
　　From the city's iconoclasm.

It a beacon light should stand,
  To point the youths of the nation
To those patriots who redeem'd our land,
  A bulwark against spoliation.

LIBERTY.

———

Liberty, we hail, we greet,
  For thee myriads have sigh'd,
To enjoy this heritage, sweet,
  Patriots have bled and died.

Nations had prostrate lain,
  In fetters firmly bound,
To break the tyrant's chain
  No potent arm was found.

A valiant chief arose,
    An illustrious son,
Who wrest'd freedom from his foes,
    'Twas the immortal Washington.

For liberty our fathers fought,
    For years in conflict bled,
They gain'd the object sought,
    We revere those patriots dead.

The people sovereign reign,
    The tyrant's rule is o'er,
Freedom was won 'mid fire and flame
    Where cannon loud did roar.

This liberty our sires gain'd,
    With noble aid from foreign lands,
A temple broad and tall was rear'd,
    That shall for ages stand.

Let liberty and law resound,
　O'er despotism roll,
Circle the globe around,
　From near to farther pole.

This liberty our fathers won,
　We will ne'er surrender,
Bequeathed from sire to son,
　Will guard it sacred ever.

Liberty, we greet, we hail,
　In its path are found no thrones,
O'er the world it will prevail,
　It knows no climes, no zones.

AWAKE, 'TIS MORN.

Awake, dearest, 'tis morn,
  The day is gently breaking,
Rise with the early dawn,
  The birds are sweetly singing.

Nature is jubilant, fairest,
  The forest is smiling,
Behold yon mountain crest,
  That Sol is gilding.

Awake, 'tis morning,
  Earth is deck'd in green,
To view scenes entrancing,
  You must rise soon.

The flowers are so ruddy,
    So fragrant their perfume,
To enjoy should rise early,
    Darling, why postpone?

While you repose in slumber,
    The dewdrop is glist'ning,
Arise, and song render,
    Yours with the bird, mingling

Dearest, you are dreaming
    Of sorrows that are past,
Awake from your sorrowing,
    To enjoy morn's rich repast.

Its nectar the gods would sip,
    With rapture would be inhaling,
While you repose in sleep,
    The nectar should be quaffing

MAPLE VALE.

———

Beneath the hills of Springfield
    A mansion lies reposing,
For scenery all to it must yield,
    So picturesque and imposing.

Sequestered amid mountains,
    This villa so lovely, so quiet, _fountains_
Environ'd 'mid forests and ~~bowers~~,
    Delight all who ~~visit~~ it. _visit_

Its arbors bloom with rare flowers,
    Their odor the air perfuming,
The resort of recluse and lovers,
    Their fragrance inhaling.

Birds of song and bright plumage,
In its groves meandering,
No place in this romantic villa
For scenery with it comparing.

On plateau tall trees o'er it wave,
O'erlooking cascades sparkling,
'Tis called Maple Vale,
For its maples stately and towering.

Its hills are deck'd so gaily,
Below a river is gliding,
'Mid environments so fairy,
Visitors delight in rambling.

This sequester'd home Elysian,
With surroundings so enchanting,
Its hostess the cultur'd Helen,
Her guests sumptuously entertaining.

May the owner of this lovely villa,
   O'er it so gracefully presiding,
And her daughter, the fair Etta,
   Like its cascades, be ever bright and sparkling.

THE MILK MAID.

———

Near a hamlet on the lawn,
  A milk maid oft was seen,
On starry eve, at dewy morn,
  Upon the crested green.

Birds carol'd notes of song,
  That echo'd o'er the hill,
The maid's was heard at early dawn,
  With the streamlet's gentle rill.

This dairy maid so lovely,
  Who in milking took delight,
When lo, a youth tall and stately
  Stood beside her one fair night.

He in dulcet tones so soft,
   Whisper'd to her, thus milking,
Darling, I love thee, have seen thee oft,
   At dewy morn and evening.

She arose, saw a youth tall and fair,
   Before him she stood offended,
As she view'd his form, his waving hair,
   Her milking she suspended.

He the offended maid did quiet,
   Caress'd and fondly kiss'd her,
These she returned with rapt delight
   That milking never gave her.

On the cottage lawn no more was seen
   This dairy maid at morn night,
She her milking pail toss'd on the green,
   Preferr'd by far her gallant knight.

TO LIZZIE.

———

Elizabeth, England's virgin Queen
   Gave to Britain power, fame,
On Afric's shore did reign
   An illustrious Queen of similar name.

Dido, who Carthage founded,
   Eliza was the name she bore,
Her gallant sons to Rome surrender'd,
   In battle fell to rise no more.

But England's trident waves
   Beyond fair Afric's bound,
It all seas doth lave,
   In all climes 'tis found.

Not all Elizas can queenly power attain,
　　Or rule o'er kingdoms, people,
But in her womanly domain
　　Her devotees are ample.

'Tis the adornment of the mind,
　　That lends the graces of attraction,
The gentle, loving, kind,
　　Receive homage, adoration.

Whate'er woman's sphere in life,
　　Humble or luxurious,
To be a mother, a devoted wife,
　　Nobler than reign Empress.

TO ETTA.

Etta, my darling Etta,
Pride of hamlet and villa,
With a face so angelic,
A form graceful, exquisite.

None so fair as my Etta,
With tresses light and wavy,
A voice sweet as zephyrs,
That falls in gentle whispers.

With my darling, my dearest,
Would roam the deep forest ;
With Etta as my own,
Would hie to some fairy home.

To ramble, mid roses and bowers,
Rare delight would be ours,
Luscious fruit would garner,
As we journey'd together.

Amid scenes enchanting,
With my Etta tarrying,
On the starry dome of night,
Would gaze with rapt delight.

In this sequester'd retreat,
To commune with nature sweet,
From this fairy forest home.
Would ne'er again roam.

There to dwell with my Etta,
Pride of hamlet and villa,
'Mid its roses and flowers
Would spend happiest of hours.

THE ROSE.

The rose, of all flowers the loveliest
That blooms in vale or forest,
So radiant, so ruddy,
So inimitable in beauty.

So delicious in odor,
Sought by recluse and lover,
The air perfum'd with its fragrance,
O'er all flowers has precedence.

It decks the temple, the altar,
The desk of savan, philosopher,
Adorns the bride, the groom,
Fairest of flowers that bloom.

Choice of Adonis and Venus,
Found in cottage and palace,
Reigns queen of the arbor,
Of the toilet, the boudoir.

Priz'd by subject, monarch,
Seen on throne, in hamlet,
Worn by orator, student,
The hero and warrior valiant.

Festoons the sculptur'd hall,
The corridors of the festive ball,
The sumptuous table graces,
Adorns the guests and pages.

Copied by Limner, artist,
Glowing with life on canvas,
Gilds the rustic home,
The ornate palatial dome.

Of all flowers the choicest,
Its fragrance the rarest,
So brilliant, so ruddy,
So radiant, so pretty.

Of love a token to Priscilla,
Resident in cottage or villa,
Emblem of constancy, purity,
Of devotion, fidelity.

The rose, so inimitable in color,
So delicious in its odor,
Delights for a season, a summer,
Its beauty departs forever.

So ruddy at dewy morn,
From its stem rudely may be torn,
At dawn fair and blooming,
Before night fading and drooping.

To mortals, the rose a picture
Of life's blooming, fading nature ;
At morn rising ruddy and radiant,
Ere night lie sleeping and silent.

TO MARY.

In the morn gathering flowers
'Mid the dew-crested bowers,
I beheld a gentle lassie,
The prettiest flower of any.

A form sylph-like, so fairy,
So queenly in her beauty,
'Mid the roses she glided,
As I gazed, was delighted.

Her eyes were sparkling,
Her smiles quite bewitching.
A face so angelic, so fair,
With bright golden hair.

Her notes fell melodious,
Soft as the lyre of Orpheus,
To music so enchanting,
Entranc'd I was list'ning.

Amid all flowers the loveliest,
Among all girls the fairest,
None can compare with Mary,
So lithe and so pretty.

Among the roses so ruddy,
I beheld this queenly beauty,
As amid them she did glide,
I strode near to her side.

As I gently approach'd her,
A kiss I stole from her.
I bade this angel good bye,
From her parted with a sigh.

At morn, 'mid the roses sweet,
I chanc'd this fairy to meet,
The brief hour we spent together,
Fond memory will recall ever.

KATY BROWN.

My charming Katy Brown,
  With a form so shapely,
The loveliest girl in town,
  So tall and so stately.

My dearest Katy Brown,
  With eyes so bewitching,
With tresses waving far down,
  They all girls surpassing.

My darling Katy Brown,
  Of you I have been dreaming,
Will you meet me on the fairy down
  On this moonlight evening?

The roses are bright and ruddy,
　　Their fragrance should be sipping
Then toss aside your books and study,
　　And with me be tripping.

Don't disappoint me, Katy Brown,
　　I will be lonely, darling,
You will find me near the lawn,
　　Don't keep me waiting.

My charming Katy Brown,
　　I love you most dearly,
Say you will be my own,
　　Answer, darling, quickly.

I wait a reply, Katy Brown,
　　So tall and so stately,
The loveliest girl in town,
　　Say yes, and I am happy.

TO A WEDDED PAIR.

The highest bliss that mortals know
  Is to be found in wedded life,
'Tis an Elysium below
  To be mated, man and wife.

To enjoy connubial bliss, the pair
  In wedlock should be mated,
For happiness in homes is rare,
  Unless hearts in love are plighted.

'Tis requited love alone
  Gives to wedded life its cheer,
It gilds the rustic home,
  It dries the falling tear.

There is nought on earth beside,
No festive hall or music sweet,
Imparts the bliss of a loving bride
And groom, who mated, fondly greet.

May it be your happy lot to enjoy
This marital bliss through life,
With no regrets, without alloy,
With your chosen, wedded wife.

THE HERMIT HOME.

On yon mountain side,
 A cottage was dimly seen,
In it a hermit did reside,
 O'er it grew the ivy green.

This home to the hermit dear,
 He long in it had dwelt,
With one to him most near,
 Who now beneath it slept.

'Twas the home of his bride,
 The bride he lov'd so well;
Their life was bliss, she died,
 No one the void could fill.

This lonely cottage home,
　The winds do o'er it glide,
No footsteps in it roam,
　Vacant its fireside.

Wintry snows sweep it o'er,
　Summer flowers still bloom,
The bridal pair ne'er more,
　Will its corridors festoon.

This home on mountain high,
　No voice in it is heard,
No note of song or sigh,
　Nought but the mocking bird.

It stands bleak and sombre,
　Once had inmates gay,
Its hosts have left it ever,
　They silent near it lay.

Bride and groom rest together,
  Ivy o'er them doth creep,
Side by side they slumber,
  On mountain crest they sleep.

OAK HALL.

In the delightful village of Clairmont,
  A unique mansion is seen,
Strangers to visit are wont,
  And partake of the luxuries within.

Environ'd 'mid roses and bowers,
  Its scenery picturesque, lovely,
In its gardens bloom rare flowers,
  Trees o'er it wave tall and stately.

This mansion, not ornate in architecture,
   Plain, but chaste in its elegance,
Admir'd by the beholder
   For its subdu'd magnificence.

This beautiful mansion,
   Its flowers fragrant, exquisite,
An ensemble of attraction,
   Delighting all who it visit.

May the fair hostess of this villa so pretty,
   Presiding o'er it so graceful,
Like its roses, be radiant and ruddy,
   Live to enjoy a happy centennial.

THE SNOW.

———

The snow, the crystal snow,
  In it youth sport and play,
Whence it comes we do not know,
  It hies from far away.

The beautiful flakes of snow,
  They bring a merry cheer,
Impart to youth a healthy glow,
  Their joyous notes we hear.

The white, fleecy snow,
  So pretty and so fairy,
Swift coursers o'er it go,
  With lads and lasses merry.

The descending flakes of snow,
  That mantles fields and hills,
Rare blessings doth bestow,
  The farmer's granary it fills.

The snow, the drifting snow,
  That piles in hillocks deep,
It fills the vales below,
  On mountain crest they sweep.

Those piles of drifted snow,
  When the sun o'er them is risen,
They melt and sweep the vale below,
  And cities lie stranded, riven.

The bright crystal snow,
  That silent falls from heaven,
May prove a friend or foe
  To mortals kindly given.

Those beautiful flakes of snow
   May bring delight or terror,
The seasons do them bestow,
   Following their pathway ever.

THE RAINBOW.

The beautiful rainbow,
   With its inimitable hue,
Circling the skies below,
   With its orange and blue.

The variegated rainbow,
   With its red, yellow and white,
Pure as the driven snow,
   Its colors so soft yet bright.

The crescent rainbow,
   Arching the heavens above,
Under it youths essay to go,
   To find some treasure trove.

The evanescent rainbow,
   To copy the artist would try,
He to nature reverent must bow,
   It all art doth defy.

The coquettish rainbow,
   Rob'd in garments so gay,
Admirers approaching, she says no,
   And prudishly hies away.

The brilliant rainbow,
   That on azure sky doth beam,
Emblem of Iris and Juno,
   Heaven's messenger and queen.

The celestial rainbow,
  Spanning the heavens o'er,
Plac'd there as a token to show
  That waters will deluge no more.

The peerless rainbow,
  How short thy dazzling reign,
Scarcely crown'd, and lo,
  Aside thy crown is lain.

Mortals, like the rainbow,
  For a brief time sparkle,
Depart whence we do not know,
  Perhaps with its rays to mingle.

THE BABE OF BETHLEHEM.

'Twas said a star brightly shone,
  O'er Bethlehem was beaming,
It onward was borne,
   O'er a babe that lay sleeping.

A brilliant noonday star,
  Rose in the heavens above,
'Twas beheld from afar,
  As a messenger of love.

By Eastern sages 'twas seen,
  At its radiance wondering,
This star that brightly did beam,
  Stood o'er an infant slumbering.

The long look'd-for Messiah
This star came to herald,
To point to the infant Saviour,
That prophets had foreshadow'd.

This babe born at Bethlehem,
As he grew maxims taught sublime,
Precursors of a millennium,
His sayings were divine.

To do good, no selfish aims in view,
The world he sought to reclaim,
For this labor'd, no rest knew,
And for his zeal was slain.

His example will not perish,
Nought can his deeds efface,
The good will them cherish,
He lived for his race.

His precepts will go down the ages,
Will inspire myriads unborn,
With the aphorisms of the sages
They all time will adorn.

AUTUMN LEAVES.

Those frosted flowers,
Symbol life's fleeting hours,
A spring an I summer gone,
A fading autumn come.

Those tinted leaves emblem
Life's unfolding problem ;
Its spring-time, summer, winter,
Its budding, fading nature.

Those leaves are drooping,
Their parent stem deserting;
They have had their life tenure,
Will bloom again never.

Those falling leaves remind us
That seasons are coursing by us,
That we, too, have had our bloom,
Our summer, our noon.

Those leaves that autumn frosted,
Our locks will have whiten'd,
And like them we must fall
To mother earth who garners all.

The leafless forest will revive
When vernal spring arrives,
But leaves that have fallen,
No power can restore them.

The seasons will course on,
Blooming flowers will come,
They from parent stem must sever,
'Tis the law of their nature.

Those flowers so beautiful in hue,
Spring will ne'er again renew,
Seasons with them are pass'd
They fall and are at rest.

So our seasons will soon be o'er,
We are approaching life's wintry shore,
Its frosts will overtake us,
No genial spring can revive us.

Those leaves emblem to mortals
That they are nearing life's portals,
That like the frosted flowers,
Will have liv'd life's fleeting hours.

THE FALLING TEAR.

The crystal falling tear,
   Life-drops of pearly dew,
Symbol affection dear
   For him she lov'd so true.

The tears that silent fall
   From moisten'd eyes,
They are garner'd all
   With the griefs and sighs.

The font from whence they flow,
   Who their depths can tell,
A mother's heart can only know,
   Who lov'd her child so well.

For her departed they are shed,
 For those she lov'd weeps,
For her darling child now dead,
 Who silent near her sleeps.

In those crystal tears we see,
 As they downward stream,
Beyond a halcyon sea,
 Where brighter skies do beam.

The glittering stars above
 Emblem those falling tears,
Symbols of unfailing love,
 Enduring as the years.

The silent tear has fallen,
 The moisten'd eyes are dry,
The sombre clouds have risen,
 Unfolding the azure sky.

Those we loved so well below
   Will ne'er to us return,
They repose where tears ne'er flow
   In mausoleum or urn.

With those we lov'd so true
   We will repose ever;
The thunder's roar, the bolt it threw
   Will arouse the sleeper never.

TO-MORROW.

The to-morrow will come,
As the hours course on,
But many great numbers
Will repose in their slumbers.

They will see no to-morrow,
But silent will lie,
Know no joy, no sorrow,
Ne'er feel a pang or sigh.

Before the to-morrow dawn,
To the mausoleum may be borne,
They no to-morrow will behold,
The shroud them will enfold.

The to-morrow to us is uncertain,

Veiled by an impenetrable curtain,

None can the to-morrow scan,

No seer, astrologer or savan.

No ken of mental prevision

Can know their to-morrow's condition,

Time present is only our own,

The future hidden, unknown.

The fleeting units of hours

Are all that are ours,

They pass by and are gone,

They will ne'er to us return.

Time, then, as it passes

On its swift-winged coursers,

We should improve as it flies,

For no to-morrow may greet our eyes.

As mortals, it behooves us

Not to neglect the time before us,

If to-morrow should not dawn,

No duties will have been left undone.

The to-morrow can hail with rejoicing,

Whatever betides its coming,

If we steadily perform our duty,

Our to-morrow, if it come, will be happy.

THE PASSING YEAR.

The year, with its hopes its fears,
    Is rapidly passing by us,
Freighted with love, joy, tears,
    Will soon have left us.

'Twill have run its round,
    None can stay its flight,
When it has reach'd its bound,
    'Twill sink in sombre night.

The years ceaseless come and go,
    On their circuits ne'er do stay,
They swiftly pass, and lo,
    Mortals lie stranded on the way.

They no joys or sorrows know,
　　Remorseless their rounds do run,
In their path the dead are found below,
　　In mausoleum and urn.

We are but waifs on life's tide,
　　That laves the near and farther shore,
As the years do o'er us glide,
　　We sink beneath, are seen no more.

The years will onward flow,
　　They course and silent fall,
Sweep o'er the high, the low,
　　The prince and monarch tall.

As we sail o'er life's stream,
　　By zephyrs gently borne,
The years pass by as a dream,
　　That fades ere 'tis morn.

We, like passing years, will slumber,
    As they do o'er us roll,
Will not hear heaven's thunder,
    That echoes from pole to pole.

This oblivious sleep will be ours
    When coursing time has o'er us fled,
Releas'd from life's cares, sorrows,
    To repose with the silent dead.

As the years onward sweep,
    Should improve as they fly,
The coming may not us greet,
    With the past will silent lie.

Present time is only ours,
    Life has but a brief tenure,
Should ne'er neglect the passing hours,
    But works perform that will perish never.

AN ELYSIUM.

Is there an Elysium when life is o'er,
   When it has ran its coursing years,
On some far-off sylvan shore,
   Or amid the distant spheres?

A serene and blissful home,
   Where we will dwell forever,
'Mid yon starry depths to roam,
   Where sorrows ne'er can enter.

Will spirits of the departed meet
   On the orbs above that glow,
And zephyrs gentle, sweet,
   Waft us to those we lov'd below

Those that before us pass'd away,

    If they yon spheres do inhabit,

Amid the myriad in space that lay,

    Shall we them find and visit?

Will we together wing our flight

    Amid empyrean heights to soar,

Where there is cloudless day, no night,

    When life on this orb is o'er.

If this Elysium shall be ours,

    'Mid the spheres to dwell for endless time,

Then swiftly pass the days, the hours,

    When we amid the stars shall shine.

THE PARTING.

We must part from those we love,
When life's brief term is o'er,
Not to meet on spheres above,
But on yon lethean shore.

There in repose will lie,
As coursing ages o'er us sweep,
Ne'er feel a pang of grief, or sigh,
As we oblivious sleep.

Our parting day will come,
Time knows no delay,
When life's race is run,
Silent we must lay.

The parting will not be long,
  We too must cross the river,
With the myriad throng,
  None can the voyage hinder.

In this silent home,
  With those we lov'd will dwell,
From it ne'er can roam,
  Amid cycles none can tell.

From this lethean shore,
  From this tomb of nature,
Will part again no more,
  But rest together ever.

WAITING.

Why don't my darling come?
  Why so long from me tarry?
Where can he have gone?
  Of waiting I am ~~tired.~~ *weary*

Hark, footsteps I hear,
  Approaching the outer door,
I think it is my dear,
  I do not hear them more.

If it is my absent darling,
  Why don't he gently knock,
And not keep me waiting?
  'Tis after one o'clock.

Oh, I am so tired,
 But I cannot sleep,
For my dearest, ador'd,
 I must vigils keep.

Why does my darling stay
 Away from me so long?
'Tis now near the break of day.
 Oh, it is. so wrong.

My eyes are red with tears,
 What has my love befallen ?
Some mishap, I have grave fears,
 Or has he me forsaken ?

The day is now dawning,
 I can no longer wait,
I must retire, sorrowing,
 How sad my fate.

So, gentle girl, take care
  How you hasty marry,
Of those youths beware
  Who revel late and early.

THE VOYAGE OF LIFE.

Man's life is fill'd with care,
  Mingl'd with joy and sorrow,
Rises blooming and fair,
  Fades ere the morrow.

His bark, with hope freight'd,
  Voyages 'mid islands fairy,
By gentle breezes wafted,
  'Mid scenes elysean does tarry.

He sails 'mid bowers of roses,
To gather he is loitering,
Until the tide he loses,
And his bark is foundering.

He is listening to sweet song,
He heeds not his danger,
Tarries and loiters too long,
Until his bark goes under.

It sinks beneath the billow,
He lies 'mid the ocean deep,
The waves are his pillow,
'Mid their refrains doth sleep.

Mortals on the ocean of life toss'd,
O'er it sail without compass or guide,
Ere the port gain'd they are lost,
Lie stranded on the tide.

Our bark to ensure a safe voyage,

　　Must be supplied with compass and oar,

If we would reach a sure anchorage,

　　The tempest ride o'er.

Nor loiter 'mid islands fairy,

　　To garner flowers by the way,

But steady pursue life's journey,

　　Until safely anchor'd we lay.

THE SPRING.

The springtime of nature,
   The gurgling streams and brooks,
Releas'd from the icy folds of winter,
   How cheerful it looks.

The snow-mantl'd hills,
   The vales and the mountains
To vernal spring yields,
   It unlocks the fountains.

The early flowers are blooming,
   The tulip and primrose are seen,
Birds are sweetly singing,
   The fields are deck'd in green.

Earth is redolent and gay,
Forest in new garments are clad,
Trees loaded with blossoms do sway,
All nature is smiling and glad.

Lovers in springtime are wooing,
Sit beneath the shady bowers,
The amours of nature viewing
In the petals and flowers.

Spring, with its inspiring forces
Restores inert nature to life,
It for all organic creatures
Provides a mate and a wife.

Spring, so ruddy and so fair,
In its coming we rejoice,
With its font of blessings rare,
Of all seasons, 'tis my choice.

LOVE.

As of love I essay to dwell,
  The muses my pen inspire,
And guide my thoughts to tell
  Whence this sacred fire.

A force, a power divine,
  It reigns supreme,
Not bound by space or time,
  Or forms of being.

For all climes 'twas made,
  From equator to far pole,
It doth the orbs pervade,
  And all worlds that roll.

Dwells in the fragrant flower,
    The tiniest mote that flies,
The eagle that on high doth tower,
    His mate far off descries.

In what sphere or place
    Did it begin its reign?
Amid what species, race?
    To enquire 'tis vain.

The muses do not know
    Where its reign began,
In which orb, above, below,
    In insect, plant, or man.

'Tis an inspiring force,
    A creative power,
Unfolds the universe,
    Gives life to the tiniest flower.

Without love life how drear,
   Earth in solitude would glide,
No homes, no welcome hear,
   Vacant the fireside.

Silent all would lie
   Oblivious in slumber,
No joy be felt, no grief, no sigh,
   Amid the realms of nature,

Fields would lose their verdure.
   No flowers to bud or bloom,
Their odor gone forever,
   No halls or corridors festoon.

No note of music heard,
   No prattling footsteps fall,
No chirp or song of bird,
   Sombre, silent all.

Love that fills the cottage home,
   Decks the earth with green,
Nature claims it for her own,
   She imperial reigns as queen.

Gives birth to all life
   On earth, the myriad spheres,
For man provides a darling wife,
   It dries the falling tears.

'Tis the font of bliss to all,
   Sweet boon of life to mortals,
Before its queenly power we fall,
   And worship at her temples.

THE FAMILY HOME.

Home, sweet home,
  What bliss is thine,
Those who have no home
  Know not its joys divine.

Nought on earth beside
  Can such bliss impart,
Here spouse and doting bride
  Are united heart with heart.

'Tis a paradise to mortals,
  Amid those homes of love,
To worship at their altars
  Symbols the home above.

Within sweet orizons ascend,
    Pæans of song arise,
Their notes in harmony blend,
    Mount to the azure skies.

Mother homes light and cheer,
    She the rustic cottage gilds,
The children to her draw near,
    Their minds with sage experience fills.

She moulds the future man,
    The wayward youth she guides,
Who can a mother's influence scan
    At the family fireside.

The early training of the child,
    When the mind is plastic, tender,
A mother's precepts mild,
    Fruit will yield ever.

Homes of love, how priz'd,
    When the family at the altar meet,
Parents by children idoliz'd,
    Listening to counsels sweet.

Such homes give pure delight,
    Flowers that parennial bloom,
They cheer the sombre night,
    Life's pathway festoon.

Amid homes abound
    The units of a nation,
The forces that republics found,
    That mark their moral station.

They are the country's shield,
    In peace or war the power,
Guard the State, the tented field,
    Protect the nation's honor.

Where homes of virtue reign,
No thieves will they create,
No vandal robbers will power attain,
Or rule the affairs of state.

Where patriot homes abound,
And youths are rightly train'd,
There elected presidents are found,
The nation's honor unstain'd.

When loving homes prevail,
In them moral precepts taught,
There republics will not fail,
Senates will ne'er be bought.

The homes of our ancestral sires,
The colonial patriots moulded,
Mothers did their sons inspire,
Who this republic founded.

This fabric we should guard with care,
  Protect with jealous honor,
Virtuous homes, a mother's prayers
  Must preserve this union ever.

THE SILENT HOME.

Gentle stranger, softly tread,
  There lie beneath your feet
Ashes of the buried dead,
  Of those who silent sleep.

No note, no voice is heard,
  Nought but the footsteps fall,
The echo of the solemn bird,
  O'er this quiet home of all.

That form of matchless grace,
  Those eyes of lustrous power,
That rivals vanquish'd in the race,
  She queen doth reign no more.

All here oblivious ~~lie,~~ *Slumber*
  He who 'mid the realms did soar,
Hears not heaven's thunder,
  Or the cyclone's fierce roar.

All beneath silent ~~slumber,~~ *lie*
  The astronomer unvailing spheres,
Unknown worlds that roll on high,
  Marks not their coursing years.

The orator with words of fire,
  Listening senators sway'd at will,
His eloquence will ne'er more inspire,
  Stark he lays and still.

Statesmen, whose prescient ken
   Republics moulded, founded,
Those great and illustrious men
   Lie beneath, enshrouded.

The geologist, delving earth,
   To learn its unfolding,
To discern its age, its birth,
   Lies in it mouldering.

Monarchs lie silent here,
   Oblivious and powerless,
Heaven's artillery do not hear,
   Their repose is endless.

The warrior drench'd in gore,
   Lays beneath, sombre,
Hears not the cannon's roar,
   The bayonet clash or sabre.

The savan studying nature's laws,
 Life's problem to discover,
Its end now knows,
 His studies have ceas'd ever.

The preacher with words that glow,
 Sinners arous'd from torpor,
Silent they rest below,
 Congregation and pastor tegether.

Those we lov'd here repose,
 As we softly near them tread,
There lie mingl'd friends and foes,
 In this home of all the dead.

Its denizens are equal,
 Prince, subject, monarch tall,
Beggar, miser, all people,
 Silent lie, powerless all.

Hark! are voices whispering?
  Are spirits hovering round?
Stranger, while you listen,
  Tread gently this sacred ground.

AMBITION.

Ambition, an inspiring power,
  A marvellous creation,
It aloft doth soar,
  Seeking high station.

What mortal can it scan,
  Its latent forces know,
That impels inert man
  To action here below.

Whence this vaulting ambition,
   Those towering aims,
This thirsting for position,
   Those longings after fame.

Where did it begin to reign?
   In what sphere or place?
Was it in yonder domain,
   Amid the angelic race?

'Twas said ambitious spirits, bold,
   That in heaven did dwell,
The standard of revolt did unfold,
   And were thrust into hell.

The brazen chariots roll'd,
   The battle echo'd round,
The rebels into Tartarus were hurl'd,
   'Mid triple walls were bound.

This ambitious rebel host
    Sought rule in heaven to gain,
In conflict with the supreme lost,
    Were doom'd to penal fires of flame.

Where do those tartarean fires glow?
    Where do they *surge* and roll?
Amid what orbs, above, below,
    Beneath equator or far pole?

Who did those fires light,
    Where rebellious spirits lie?
Who were worst'd in the fight,
    Was it he who rules on high?

Were those ceaseless fires of flame
    Kindled by the supreme,
To torture with endless pain,
    Those to whom he gave being?

Those powers the creator does bestow
Upon the dwellers in yon domain,
He their ambitious aims did know,
Or he omniscient did not reign.

The gods who rule are just,
The habitats of earth, of myriad spheres,
Their magna mater can trust,
Of tartarean fires have no fears.

HOPE.

——

Hope gives to life its cheer,
Lightens its burdens, cares,
To mortals kindly given,
Or who could suffer being.

Amid the storms of life,
Its ills, sorrows, strife,
Hope beholds a brighter day,
It lights our dreary way.

Beyond the clouds are seen
Stars that brightly beam,
The murky vapors rise,
Reveal the azure skies.

Hope, a font, whose sylvan flow
Festoons our path below
With flowers that perennial bloom,
That shed on life a sweet perfume.

As o'er the stream of life we sail,
Hope knows no such word as fail,
It manfully applies the oar,
Safely to ride the tempest o'er.

Though storm-toss'd and riven,
Hope views a halcyon haven,
Which he seeks to enter,
Within securely ride at anchor.

As o'er mountain crest we travel,
On distant vistas revel,
Scenes elysian, fairy,
Cheer us as we journey.

Hope builds a palatial home,
With ornate corridors and dome,
Its arbors bloom with fragrant flowers,
In which to while the passing hours.

This gorgeous home, so lovely,
Pictur'd to our fancy,
Away this airy home it flies,
It ne'er will greet our mortal eyes,

In life's declining years,
Hope to be devout, oft at prayers,
To give liberally to pious uses,
And thus atone for long abuses.

The gods who rule above, below,
On the worthy their gifts bestow,
Not pious uses nor saintly parsons
Will secure us tranquil havens.

To meet life's rude encounter,
Hope and effort must go together,
By these the port we can gain,
Hope alone, how vain.

This expectant haven we can enter
By honest toil, moral culture,
Pretentious zeal, priestly lore
Will strand our bark on rocky shore.

To gain entrance to this harbor,
In it ride secure at anchor,
We the bark must man, must guide,
If we would o'er life's tempest ride.

To enter this halcyon haven,
From false guides must be ridden,
With honest effort apply the oar,
The gods are just, require no more.

TIME.

Time, thou art master,
  Supreme thou dost reign,
O'er every living creature,
  Within thy vast domain.

Thou hadst a beginning,
  'Mid the depths of the past,
Will ne'er have an ending
  While the universe lasts.

When orbs in space were hurl'd,
  Began their circling round
As they onward whirl'd,
· Thou didst them bound.

Thou mark'dst their flight
   As they cours'd their way
'Mid the solitudes of night,
   Ere there was dawn or day.

Before life on the spheres there came,
   Thou didst their pathway trace,
As they revolv'd in fire and flame,
   Amid the realms of space.

To register time there was none,
   There were no recorded pages,
'Mid empyrean heights alone,
   The orbs cours'd for ages.

As cycles onward roll'd,
   The earth gave birth to man,
As he science did unfold,
   Her orbital time did scan.

Nought before time can stand,
   He hath imperial sway,
He sweeps o'er ocean, land,
   And myriads prostrate lay.

Beneath him there repose
   All forms of life and being,
He no friend or foe knows,
   None his eye escaping.

Before his relentless scythe there lie,
   The countless dead that sleep,
They lay pil'd mountains high,
   Beneath his hoary sweep.

Since Saturn's reign on earth began,
   He to none hath shown favor,
All forms of life to imperial man
   Have fallen before this mighty slayer.

TO A WEDDED WIDOW.

Arise, my love, 'tis morn,
 And quaff its inspiring glow ;
Perhaps you dream of days forlorn,
 And years of wedded woe.

Arise to happier days,
 Dreams will no more disturb you,
Nought shall chill those genial rays,
 Inspired by love so true.

The shades of night have sped,
 Apollo yon mountain gilds,
Knox before his rays have fled,
 He lights the vales and hills.

Rise with the blush of dawn,
  Sol's early beams to greet,
With the birds unite your song,
  With notes of music sweet.

Rise, behold the pearly dew,
  Like diamonds o'er the fields,
The skies of azure blue,
  The streamlet's gentle rills.

Arise, the hills are deck'd in bloom,
  No more of sorrows dream,
Darling, do not repose till noon,
  You miss the enchanting scene.

A WELL-SPENT LIFE.

An old man, bow'd and gray,
  Frost'd by four score years,
As on dying couch he lay,
  To pass the vale had no fears.

His voyage of life was o'er,
  He had weather'd its storm;
Calm he view'd the lethean shore,
  On gentle zephyrs borne.

He felt life's ebbing tide,
  As yon port he was nearing,
On works, not faith, relied
  To reach its tranquil haven.

His benevolence was broad,
 He had no pretentious zeal,
Pamper'd not pious fraud,
 Who pray, but no vices heal.

His cottage door was open,
 The deserving did not turn away,
What he had was freely given,
 With gifts, kind words did say.

The promises he made
 With fidelity were kept,
To do the right was not afraid,
 Oft for the afflicted wept.

He rail'd not at foibles,
 But vices did rebuke:
He had no disguises,
 The highest good he sought.

He liv'd to benefit his race,
His hands unstain'd with lucre,
Sought not power, place,
Kept unblemish'd his honor.

He beheld a deity
In yonder starry dome,
That deck'd the earth with beauty,
A magnificence her own.

The tiny summer flower,
The mighty spheres that roll,
Symbol'd to him a power,
That all things control.

He worship'd in no temple,
Bow'd before no altar,
Under nature's dome, ample,
Sang orisons and psalter.

His kindly acts will not perish,
   Flowers that perennial bloom,
The good them will cherish,
   Life's pathway will festoon.

They will go down the ages,
   Live in the coming future,
Add a ripple to life's pages,
   That will flow on ever.

The gods the worthy know,
   The good will forget never,
On those their gifts bestow,
   Who equivalents render.

The scales are justly held,
   The balances are proven,
Their judgments ne'er sold,
   Decrees are rightly given.

A tribunal of last resort,
    From it lies no appeal,
Verdicts are never bought,
    Gold is of no avail.

Nature is always true
    To the children she bore,
They who the right pursue,
    Are safe, she asks no more.

www.ingramcontent.com/pod-product-compliance
Lightning Source LLC
Chambersburg PA
CBHW032008060726
47497CB00017B/2398